# All About Allergies

## Also by Susan Neiburg Terkel

Ethics

Abortion: Facing the Issues
Feeling Safe, Feeling Strong (with Janice Rench)
Honest Abe
Should Drugs Be Legalized?
Understanding Child Custody
Yoga Is for Me

# All About Allergies

by Susan Neiburg Terkel

illustrated by Paul Harvey

**Lodestar Books**
Dutton ✳ New York

*Library of Congress Cataloging-in-Publication Data*

Terkel, Susan Neiburg.
  All about allergies / by Susan Neiburg Terkel; illustrated
by Paul Harvey.—1st ed.
      p.  cm.
  Includes bibliographical references and index.
  Summary: Provides information about different kinds of
allergies, and their symptoms, diagnoses, and treatments.
  ISBN 0-525-67410-1
  1. Allergy—Juvenile literature.  [1. Allergy.]
I. Harvey, Paul, 1926–  ill.  II. Title.
RC585.T47   1993
616.97—dc20                                    92-17770
                                                  CIP
                                                  AC

Published in the United States by Lodestar Books,
an affiliate of Dutton Children's Books,
a division of Penguin Books USA Inc.,
375 Hudson Street, New York, New York 10014

Published simultaneously in Canada by
McClelland & Stewart, Toronto

Editor: Rosemary Brosnan    Designer: Richard Granald/LMD

Printed in the U.S.A.    First Edition
10  9  8  7  6  5  4  3  2  1

**to Dave Terkel**

*The author would like to thank the following people for their help with this book:*
*Alexandra Clegg, Ben Cox, Debbie Crotteau, Dr. Sidney Davidow,*
*Dr. Philip Fleekop, Alison Furman, Ruth Furman, Dr. Steven Johnson,*
*Margie Origlio, Bobby Pelander,*
*Dr. Howard Schwartz, Jane Spencer, Dave Terkel,*
*and Mary Alice Wilkens.*

# Contents

# ❋❋*1*❋❋

# Ah-choo!

When Tyler eats strawberries, he itches and itches. Red bumps break out all over his skin.

If Jennifer pets a dog, snuggles with a cat, or rides a horse, her eyes tear and her throat gets dry and scratchy.

When Jamie plays outdoors among the trees, weeds, and grass, he sneezes, wheezes, and coughs.

Even Jamie's dog itches at the smell of cut grass.

**What Is an Allergy?**

It is normal to cough near smoke. It is normal to scratch your back when you are wearing an itchy wool sweater. And if you

have a cold, it is normal to have a runny nose and teary eyes, and to sneeze a lot.

It is also normal to eat berries, get close to animals, and smell cut grass *without* sneezing, coughing, itching, wheezing, or breaking out in hives.

Allergies are like having the wrong opinion about a person you know, like mistaking someone who is a true friend for an enemy. When people with allergies come in contact with certain foods, dust, pollens, drugs, or other things that are normally harmless, their bodies act as though these substances are harmful.

## Enemies Now

Anything that causes an allergic reaction is called an allergen. If Joshua gets bitten by too many mosquitoes, hives break out all over his skin. Therefore, for Joshua, mosquitoes are an allergen.

Almost anything we breathe, touch, eat, or take into our bodies can be an allergen. That is why people who are prone to allergies can be sensitive to a long list of allergens!

4

For many people, though, the list of allergens is short.

Some people are allergic to certain foods. Common food allergens are milk, eggs, shellfish, nuts, peas, soybeans, strawberries, tomatoes, and chocolate.

Some people are allergic to things they breathe. Common airborne allergens are plant pollens, spores, and dust.

Some people are allergic to insect stings. Common insect allergens include the venom of bees, wasps, yellow jackets, and hornets. (Venom is the fluid in the sting that is poisonous.)

Some people are allergic to drugs. Common drug allergens are penicillin, a drug used to fight infection, and aspirin.

Some people are allergic to things they touch. Common skin allergens are poison ivy and poison oak, certain metals like nickel, detergents, and cosmetics.

## As Time Goes By

Allergies caused by plant pollens last only as long as the plant's pollinating season. Because plant pollens cause so many people's allergies, the different growing seasons are often referred to as "allergy season."

## Ah-choo!

Ari is allergic to tree pollen. Every spring, when the leaves of oak, maple, birch, and other trees start to bloom and their pollen fills the air, Ari's eyes itch and tear. Thus, for Ari, spring is "allergy season."

Sometimes a person has two or three allergy seasons. Jessica has allergies to grass pollens that fill the air from April to July. She is also allergic to ragweed pollen, which is in the air from August until the first frost.

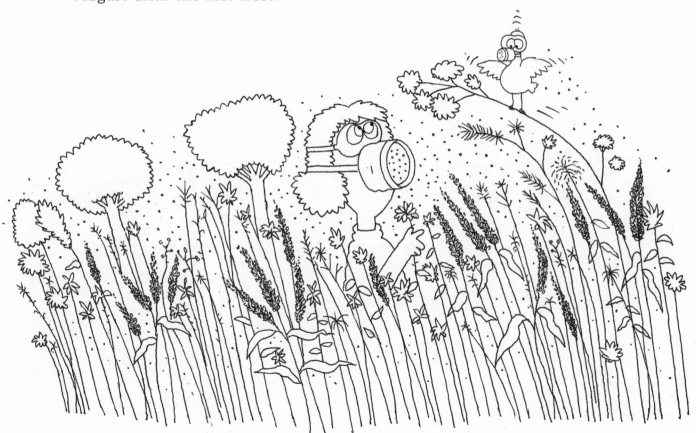

Some allergies are year-round. That's because the allergen is always in the air.

Brittany is allergic to dust. No matter how hard she and her family try to keep their house dust-free, there is always some dust in the air. So, all year long, Brittany has allergies.

# ✳✳ **2** ✳✳

# Making Mistakes

Some children dislike broccoli.

Practically everyone dislikes the smell of skunks. But neither is an allergy. Nor is it an allergy to dislike homework or taking out the trash—although you may think you are "allergic" to homework or chores.

For something to be an allergy, the body's immune system has to do the disliking.

**Looking Out for Number One**
Our immune system protects us from germs and other harmful invaders that enter our body and make us sick. It also protects

us from enemies that the body makes itself, such as tumors. Indeed, without an immune system, we would not be able to stay well.

Within the immune system are white blood cells that produce antibodies. These antibodies fight germs and harmful invaders.

Many different kinds of antibodies exist, each of which works against its own specific enemy invader.

Antibodies are a protein substance called immunoglobulin, or Ig for short. There are five basic types of Ig: G, M, A, D, and E.

The first kind, IgG, is the most common type. In fact, three-fourths of all antibodies belong to this group. If we get the flu, IgG antibodies fight off the germs that caused it. If we scrape our knee, they rush to the scrape to fight off infection.

Scientists aren't sure, but they think that the last kind—IgE—defends our body against tiny worms and bugs, called parasites, that get into it. When people go barefoot all the time or eat certain foods that are raw or aren't well cooked, like sushi, they can get parasites.

## Too Much of a Good Thing?

Compared to the amount of IgG we have, we have very little IgE. Even so, people with allergies appear to have more IgE than people without allergies.

If IgE antibodies help the body stay well, and if people with allergies have more of it, then what's the problem? The problem is that IgE is prone to making mistakes!

In people with allergies, IgE antibodies mistake things that are normal as being harmful. The first time an allergen enters the body, IgE antibodies don't do much. But afterward, maybe many times later, they make the mistake of judging something delicious like ice cream as harmful. Or they may think that playing with kittens and puppies is bad.

Most IgEs are found in the parts of the body that help you breathe—your nose, throat, and lungs—the parts that help you digest food—your stomach and intestines—and in your skin.

In these places, mast cells are also found. Mast cells are everywhere in our body, but especially in the nose, lungs, throat, and skin.

## Making Mistakes

IgE antibodies are shaped like a **Y**. On the outside of the mast cells are places where the stem of the **Y** fits.

The arms of the IgE antibody fit together with the allergen. In fact, IgEs and allergens fit together perfectly, like pieces of a jigsaw puzzle.

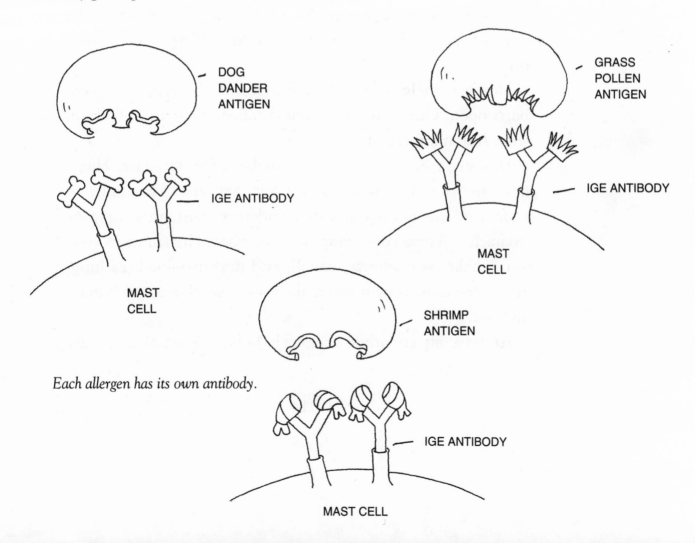

DOG DANDER ANTIGEN

IGE ANTIBODY

MAST CELL

GRASS POLLEN ANTIGEN

IGE ANTIBODY

MAST CELL

SHRIMP ANTIGEN

IGE ANTIBODY

MAST CELL

*Each allergen has its own antibody.*

Different IgE antibodies match different allergens. For example, an IgE antibody that matches milk allergen is different from the IgE antibody that matches grass pollen allergen.

## Matching Up

IgEs work in pairs. When there is a matching allergen, the arms of both IgEs fit together with the allergen to form a bridge.

Heavy with IgEs and their bridges of allergen, mast cells burst open. Out comes a chemical called histamine. And oh, what histamine can do!

Histamine in your throat will make it feel scratchy. Histamine in your nose will make it itch and run. Histamine in your eyes will make them itch and tear. Histamine in your stomach will give you cramps and diarrhea. Histamine in your lungs makes you wheeze, cough, and have trouble breathing. Histamine in your skin will make it itch, swell, and get bumpy and red.

At least fifteen other chemicals besides histamine usually

## Making Mistakes

join the battle to fight allergens. If enough histamine and other chemicals are released, you can feel very ill.

If only the IgEs weren't so mistaken!

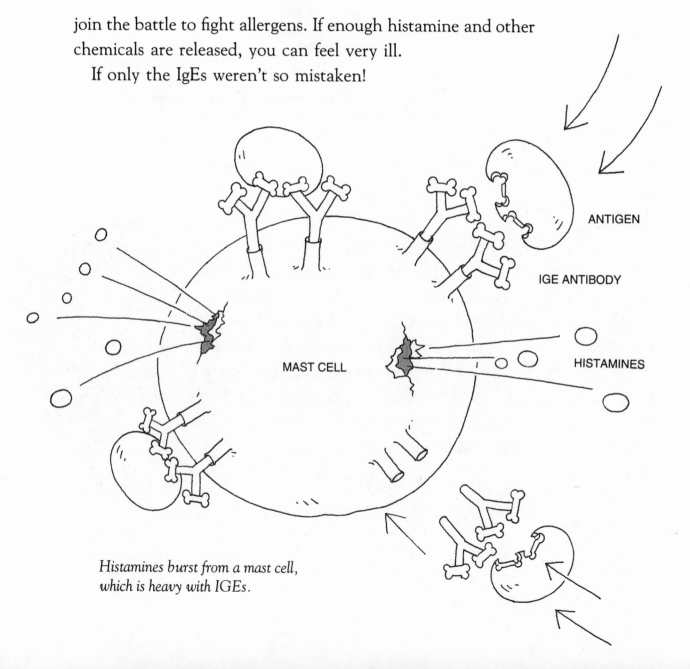

ANTIGEN

IGE ANTIBODY

MAST CELL

HISTAMINES

*Histamines burst from a mast cell, which is heavy with IGEs.*

# ✳✳ 3 ✳✳

# Sooner or Later

Once the body has learned to make an IgE to exactly fit a specific allergen, it will remember how to do it again. Then, whenever that kind of allergen enters the body, IgEs will be mass-produced to fit it—and fight it!

When enough IgEs form allergen bridges on enough mast cells, which are releasing enough histamine and other chemicals, sooner or later you will have an allergic reaction. A reaction occurs when the histamine and other chemicals go to work and cause allergy symptoms.

**Overload**

Peter had a dog. At first his IgE ignored Skipper. After a while, though, his immune system decided Skipper was too much dog in Peter's life. That's when Peter had his first allergy attack.

With histamine released in his nose and eyes, his nose ran, his eyes teared, and he sneezed every time he was near Skipper—even every time he was near where Skipper *had been*.

Sometimes the immune system will put up with a dog when no other allergen is present. But if a second allergen enters the body, the immune system may get "overloaded" and will often react to both of them.

For example, Lauren had a dog that she was never allergic to. Her best friend, Cassie, had a cat, to which Lauren was not allergic either. But when Cassie brought the cat to stay with Lauren while she and her family went on vacation, the cat and dog together caused Lauren to sneeze, wheeze, and wish Cassie would return.

## Smooth Sailing

When you are rested and feeling fine, your immune system is least likely to make you sick from allergies. But when you get sick, overtired, very unhappy, or quite nervous, your immune system doesn't work as well—and frequently makes your allergic reactions worse.

We can't always be rested, healthy, or happy. Even then, many people still have allergies. But to help your allergies, it is worth trying to be that way—though not at the risk of becoming a couch potato. Some of our best Olympic athletes have allergies, and that doesn't stop them from exercising or achieving athletic success.

# *** 4 ***

# Who Gets Allergies?

The good news is that most people do not have enough IgEs to cause allergies. This is small comfort, though, to the millions of people who do.

Nor does everyone with a lot of IgEs have allergy symptoms. Before the immune system mass-produces antibodies, it must first make a blueprint.

Sometimes the immune system meets the allergen only once, mass-producing IgEs to match it at the next meeting. Often, several meetings are necessary before an allergic reaction takes place.

For example, if Danielle eats a lot of shellfish, she would become allergic to it, as she has IgEs that match shellfish. But her family is vegetarian, and Danielle eats no shellfish. And until she does, she remains free of an allergy to shellfish.

## The Family Tree

You can't catch allergies the way you catch chicken pox or a common cold. However, you can inherit them from your parents or grandparents.

Chances are, if no one in your family has allergies, you won't either. But if one of your parents does, and especially if both of them do, you have a greater chance of getting allergies sometime in your life.

Occasionally, allergies skip a generation or two. So while your parents may not pass on allergies, you can still get them from a grandparent or even a great-grandparent. Certainly there are better gifts to pass on. But no one passes on allergies deliberately.

# Who Gets Allergies?

## Like and Unlike

Tommy's father laughs hardest when he watches his favorite TV show. Tommy doesn't think the show is funny, but when the dog chases his tail, Tommy gets hysterical.

Allergies are no joke, and like humor in a family, they vary from person to person. Thus, your father could be allergic to cats and grass, while you can be allergic to dogs and honeybees.

### Even Dogs Have Allergies

People are not the only ones to get allergies. Dogs, especially poodles, suffer from allergies too.

Remember Jamie's dog—who itched every time she smelled cut grass? Like many people, Jamie's dog is allergic to grass pollen. Instead of sneezing from grass pollen, as people usually do, she gets itchy skin from it.

Until a veterinarian gave her a pill to stop the itching, Jamie's dog scratched all day and night during allergy season.

# ✳✳ 5 ✳✳

# How Do You Know if You Have Allergies?

If you have already had an allergy attack, you know you have an allergy.

But symptoms like wheezing, sneezing, hives, and itching cannot always be blamed on allergies. Instead, they may be caused by colds or other illnesses.

A good doctor can find out whether or not your symptoms are caused by allergies. This doctor may be your family doctor or pediatrician, a doctor who treats only children. Or this doctor may be someone who has studied the immune system and knows a lot about allergies. Such doctors are called allergists.

Doctors have several ways of finding out if you have allergies.

## A Careful Look at You

The first thing a good allergy doctor does is take a careful look at you. The doctor will look up your nose and in your eyes and ears. He or she will listen to your heart and lungs.

Your doctor will also ask you many questions, such as:

- Does your nose run and do your eyes itch every spring or summer (a clue to seasonal allergies)?
- Does it feel like something is always dripping down your throat?
- Do you cough a lot, even when you don't feel sick?
- Do you always feel sick to your stomach or get diarrhea when you eat certain foods?
- Do you ever have difficulty breathing?

## How Do You Know if You Have Allergies?

- Does your skin ever itch or get red bumps on it?
- You will even be asked if your ears ever itch!
- And the most important question: What do *you* think you are allergic to?

Asking such questions and writing down their answers is called taking a history.

After the examination and the medical history are finished, your doctor will have a clue to whether or not you have allergies and, if so, what they are.

## Only Skin Deep

If your doctor needs more clues, he or she might test you for allergies. Because there is so much IgE near your skin, a skin test can detect if you are allergic to certain things.

With a little prick or scratch, which hurts just a bit, a tiny amount of allergen enters your skin. Or the doctor may put a patch on your skin that has allergen on it. Then your skin absorbs the allergen on the patch.

Dr. Johnson scratched some egg allergen on Ben's back. She scratched bee allergen on another place. Nothing happened where the egg allergen was scratched. But where the bee allergen was, Ben felt itchy, and a welt appeared. From the test, Ben learned that he is allergic to bees, but not eggs.

The tiny amount of allergen used in these tests may not be enough to trigger an allergic reaction. Yet even without a reaction, the doctor may still suspect that you are allergic to that specific allergen.

To confirm this, the doctor uses a larger amount of allergen. This larger amount is injected under the skin, instead of merely scratched into it.

## In the Lab

Another kind of allergy test is done in a lab. It is called the radio allergoserbent test (RAST).

Here, some of your blood is mixed with different allergens in a test tube. Then someone who is specially trained to detect IgE reactions studies the mixture to see if anything occurs.

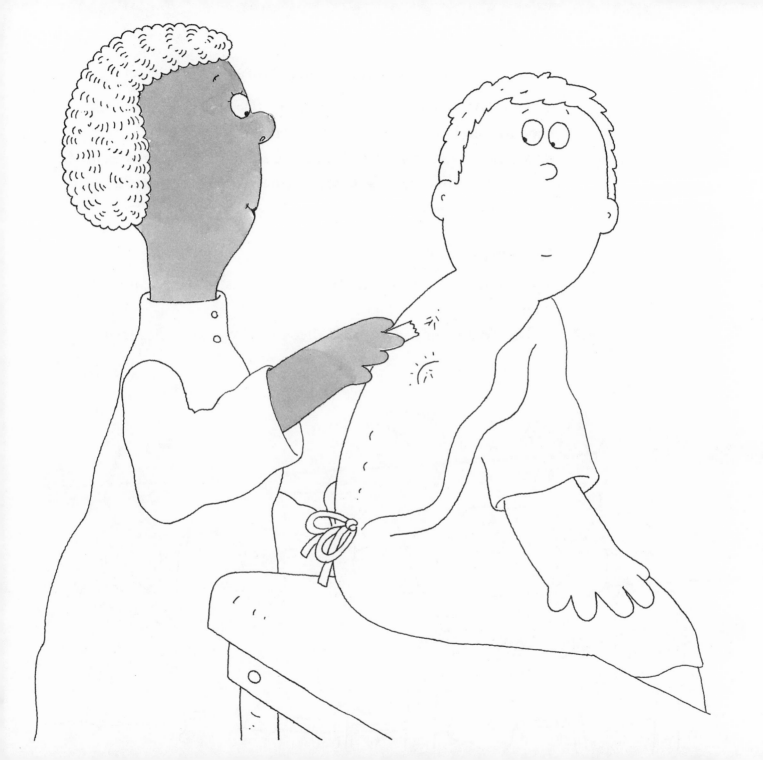

The RAST is not used very often. Because it takes a long time to watch for allergic reactions in the lab, this test is slow and expensive to conduct. And since so many more IgEs exist in the skin than in the blood, skin tests are better allergy detectives anyway.

## Watch What You Eat

Still another way to learn about allergies is to study carefully what you eat.

The doctor may give you a diet to follow. This diet means

that for a while you stop eating all the foods that the doctor suspects are causing your allergies.

Then you eat a new food that was missing from the diet. If it gives you an allergic reaction, you know it is an allergen for you. If it doesn't, you eat it another day or two and see what happens. After you decide whether or not that food causes your allergies, you try another new food.

One by one, you try out all the foods you had stopped eating when you began the diet. In this way, you learn which foods cause your allergies and which foods are safe to eat.

# **\*\*6\*\* Treating Allergies**

Once you learn the allergens to which you are sensitive, the doctor can show you how to treat your allergies.

### Hide and Seek

The best way to treat allergies is to stay away from the substances that cause them.

Alexandra is so sensitive to peanuts that if she eats even *one*, her immune system gets very busy and does a lot of harm.

By not eating peanuts—or anything made with them—she avoids allergy attacks. This means that she also does not eat peanut candy, peanut butter, peanut butter cookies, or even potato chips that are fried in peanut oil.

## Treating Allergies

To avoid peanuts, Alexandra has learned to read the labels on food, which list everything in that food. That way, if one of the ingredients is peanuts or is made from peanuts, she won't eat that food.

She has also learned to ask about food that is offered to her. "Is this made with peanuts or peanut products?" she asks whenever she is unsure whether the food served to her contains peanuts.

Even after reading labels and asking, Alexandra may still be unsure if a food contains any peanut products. So she avoids the food altogether, because even a small peanut can give her a big reaction.

Not all allergens can be avoided, however.

Ryan is allergic to dust mites, which are tiny insects found dead or alive in most house dust.

Dust mites collect on carpets and feather pillows. Ryan tries to avoid them by sleeping in a room with a wooden floor. His pillow is made of polyester. By avoiding dust mites as much as possible, Ryan is able to control his allergies somewhat. Still, dust mites are in the air all the time, so Ryan has allergies—all the time.

## Fighting Back

Although you can't always avoid allergens, your allergy symptoms can be treated.

Because the main cause of allergic reaction is histamine, many allergic people take a drug that stops histamine from doing harm. This drug is called an antihistamine.

## Treating Allergies

During allergy season, people with allergies may take antihistamines every day. That way, their bodies are ready to fight off histamine as soon as an allergy attack begins.

Those people who don't come in contact with their allergens every day usually wait for an allergic attack before taking an antihistamine or other allergy medicine.

Some people treat their allergy symptoms locally—at the place in the body where the reaction is occurring. During allergy season, Nathan's eyes itch and tear. To control his itching and tearing, he uses eye drops that have medicine in them.

For a few people, an allergic attack can be so severe that it threatens the lungs and heart. When this occurs, these people require emergency medical care and strong drugs.

To alert anyone who assists them during a severe allergy attack, extremely allergic people sometimes wear necklaces or bracelets with information about their allergy.

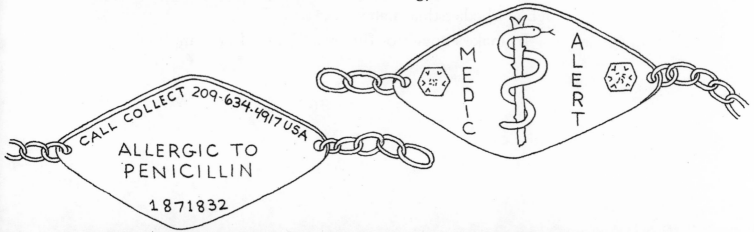

Daniel is so allergic to bee stings that even one sting can be terrible for him. As a result, whenever he goes outdoors in spring or summer, he takes his treatment along with him. And he always wears a Medic Alert necklace.

## Enlisting the Good Guys

Still another treatment is allergy shots.

Often, the immune system will ignore a tiny bit of allergen. This gives the IgG antibodies—the antibodies that do most of the immune system's protective work—a chance to match the allergen before the IgE antibodies do.

When IgG antibodies bind with an allergen, they don't hook onto a mast cell. In this way, they avoid releasing histamine and causing an allergic reaction.

Even though large amounts of IgG are already in the body, in order to outnumber the IgE antibodies for a particular allergen, you need more IgG that matches the allergen than the IgE antibodies that match it.

To make enough of the exact kind of IgG antibodies you

## Treating Allergies

need, you are injected with a small amount of allergen once or twice a week. (If too much were injected at a time, the immune system would not be fooled.)

As the IgG antibodies increase in number, larger amounts of allergen can be injected. When you build up enough IgG to "outsmart" your IgE, you can come in contact with an allergen without having an allergy attack.

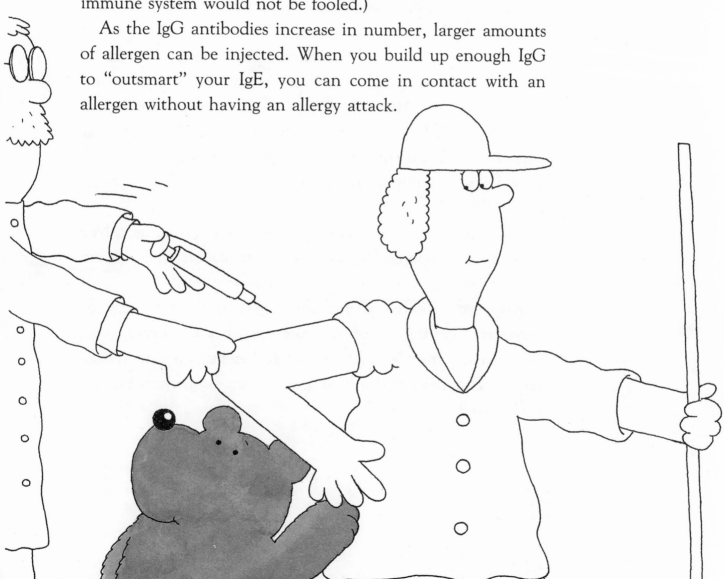

It can take months to build up IgGs before you notice any help from the shots. And you will probably need shots for several years before you have enough IgGs to beat all your IgEs to the job.

Lizzie wanted to be able to hike outdoors without sneezing. She was so allergic to pollen that she could never go hiking with her friends. After a few years of allergy shots, Lizzie had enough pollen IgG to overcome her pollen IgE. When that happened, she was finally able to enjoy the outdoors, even on a dry, sunny day in the fall when there was a lot of pollen in the air.

Not everyone who gets allergy shots can fool their IgEs. Nor have drug companies learned yet to make serum for every single allergy.

And even though allergy shots may help, not everyone agrees that getting a shot or two every week for several years is worth the trouble. They would rather put up with the allergies. That is a decision you have to make with your parents and doctor.

## Growing Up

For some people, growing up means growing out of their allergies. For others, allergies worsen with age, and new allergies appear.

And to help everyone with allergies, children and grown-ups alike, researchers around the world are looking for new and better ways to treat allergies.

# ✳✳ 7 ✳✳

# Where Are All the Allergies?

What you have just learned about allergies should help you understand the ones that you or someone you know has. This chapter offers a short list of the most common allergies people get.

**Hay Fever**

Hay fever does not really come from hay. Nor does it cause a fever. It was named hay fever at a time when doctors knew nothing about allergies. They mistook all the sneezing and coughing that some people had each growing season for the common cold.

As we learned earlier, hay fever comes from the tiny grains of pollen that are carried from plant to plant in the air. Although many people are allergic to tree and grass pollen, the most common allergy is to ragweed pollen.

Ragweed grows in many places, but it is found mostly in fields and empty lots. Its growing season is from August until the first frost, which usually occurs by October or November.

If you are allergic to ragweed, you will have a hard time avoiding the pollen. That's because a single ragweed plant makes a million grains of pollen in one day, and about 8 *billion* in one season. Not only that, the pollen is so light, the wind can carry it great distances—even hundreds of miles.

During hay fever season, pollen counts are taken. A sample of air is checked to see how many grains of pollen are in it. This information is reported in the newspaper or on television. When the weather is sunny and dry, the pollen count

## Where Are All the Allergies?

can climb very high. In contrast, rain takes much of the pollen out of the air. So people with hay fever may actually look forward to bad weather!

## Asthma

Another common allergy is asthma.

Although asthma may be caused by the flu, too much exercise, or by breathing air that is too cold, it is often caused by allergies.

During an asthma attack, mast cells in the lungs blast off histamine and other chemicals. The histamine squeezes tight the tubes that carry air from the nose and mouth to the air sacs in the lungs. It also causes the air sacs to fill with mucus. This tightness and extra mucus cause coughing, wheezing, and problems with breathing—symptoms that can be scary at times.

There are many ways to treat asthma, depending on how severe an attack is. Among the most popular treatments are drugs that people inhale (breathe in) as soon as they feel an attack coming on. The medicine they inhale relaxes their bronchial tubes, allowing them to breathe easily again.

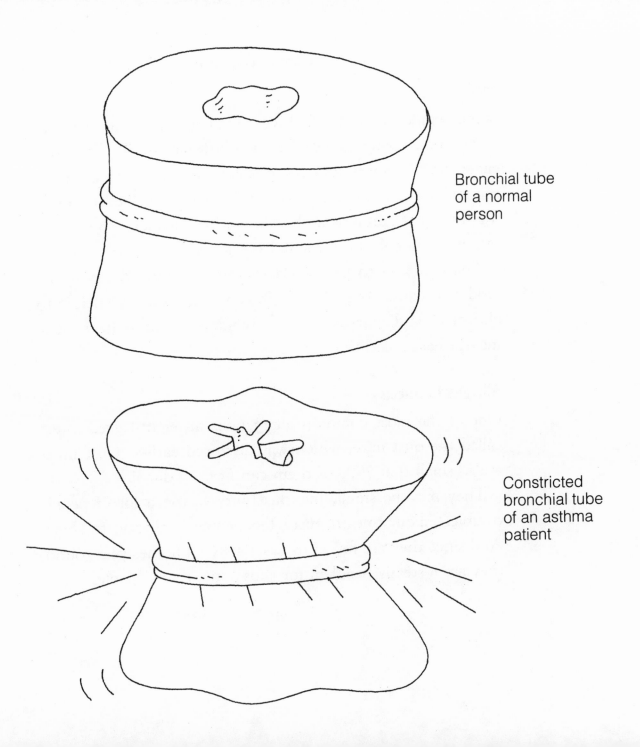

Bronchial tube
of a normal
person

Constricted
bronchial tube
of an asthma
patient

## Food Allergies

Some people break out in hives whenever they eat tomatoes or peaches. Other people feel their throats swell when they eat shellfish. Others get stomachaches or diarrhea from drinking milk or eating cheese. Still others get headaches from eating food that contains additives—added chemicals to make it tastier, more colorful, or stay fresh longer.

The best way to treat food allergies is to avoid eating the food that causes the allergy. Of course, if you are allergic to chocolate and dairy products, avoiding a chocolate sundae may be easier said than done!

## Allergies to Insects

One of the most common allergens is an eight-legged insect called the dust mite, which was discussed earlier. Dust mites are so small that 7000 of them can fit on a dime!

They may be small, but dust mites cause a lot of people trouble. About one in every ten people is allergic to them. And since they are found in practically all homes year-round, they are a steady problem for those one in ten people.

## Where Are All the Allergies?

Other common insect allergens come from the family of bees, wasps, hornets, yellow jackets, and certain ants that inject venom when they sting their victims. For people who are quite allergic to these insects, the stings cause more than just pain. They cause histamine to go everywhere in the body, which can be a major medical problem.

## Allergies to Animals

Most people think that an animal's fur causes allergies. Actually, what causes them is the animal's dander—the flakes of dead skin that an animal sheds.

Being allergic to a beloved pet can be especially difficult to accept. Danny loved his cat. Unfortunately, when he developed asthma, he had to find another home for it. Even though Danny found a good home for his cat, he was very sad.

## Other Allergies

Many people are allergic to drugs like penicillin or aspirin. Until they have an allergic reaction to a drug, however, they have no way of predicting a drug allergy.

Skin allergies give people reactions to something they touch. After coming into contact with detergents, cleansers, chemicals, or plants such as poison ivy, their skin gets itchy and red. Such allergies are quite common among babies and toddlers who wear diapers.

Ever notice the mold that grows on stale bread? Throughout the year, except when snow is on the ground, similar molds grow on wheat, corn, oats, grass, leaves, and soil. These molds release billions of spores into the air. Many people are allergic to the spores, which they breathe in from the air. In fact, molds are one of the biggest causes of seasonal allergies.

It can take a lot of detective work to find the cause of a particular allergic reaction. And sometimes, the cause remains a mystery—to all but the person's immune system, which recognizes it instantly!

# Glossary

**allergen** a substance that causes an allergic reaction

**allergist** a doctor who specializes in treating allergies

**allergic reaction** the body's response when the immune system attacks an allergen

**allergy** unpleasant reaction to certain foods, pollens, animals, and other things

**allergy attack** a severe allergic reaction

**antibody** a cell in the body that destroys or weakens germs and toxins

**antihistamine** a drug that helps the body deal with too much histamine

**asthma** a condition in which breathing becomes difficult because of mucus in the air sacs of the lungs and tightening of the tubes that carry air from the nose and mouth to the lungs

**examination** what happens when the doctor carefully looks at your body to see what is causing your symptoms

51

**hay fever** allergy to ragweed pollen

**histamine** a chemical in the body that is released during an allergy attack; too much histamine causes itching, sneezing, wheezing, and other symptoms

**IgE** antibody that causes allergies

**IgG** antibody that does much of the immune system's work, fighting infection and disease

**immune system** the body's way of protecting us from harmful germs

**mast cell** a cell in the body that stores histamine and other chemicals

**penicillin** a drug used to fight infection

**RAST** a blood test used to detect allergies

**symptom** a change in the body that indicates that illness is present

**tumor** an abnormal mass of tissue

**venom** the poisonous fluid in an insect or animal sting

# Further Reading

Berger, Melvin. *Germs Make Me Sick*. New York: Thomas Y. Crowell, 1985.

Burns, Sheila. *Allergies and You*. New York: Julian Messner, 1980.

Newman, Nanette. *That Dog*. New York: Thomas Y. Crowell, 1983.

Seixas, Judith. *Allergies: What They Are, What They Do*. New York: Greenwillow Books, 1991.

Silverstein, Dr. Alvin, and Silverstein, Virginia B. *Allergies*. New York: J. B. Lippincott, 1977.

You can write and ask for pamphlets from:

American Academy of Allergy and Immunology
611 East Wells Street
Milwaukee, Wisconsin 53202

Information Office
National Institute of Allergy and Infectious Diseases
9000 Rockville Pike
Bethesda, Maryland 20892-0001

# Index

Page numbers in *italics* refer to illustrations.

# Index

# INDEX

# Index

## About the Author

SUSAN NEIBURG TERKEL is the author of several well-received books for young people, including *Ethics* and *Abortion: Facing the Issues*. She holds a degree in Child Development and Family Relationships from Cornell University.

Ms. Terkel lives in Hudson, Ohio, with her husband and three children, all of whom are "allergic" to household chores.

## About the Illustrator

PAUL HARVEY lives in Westport, Connecticut. He has done many illustrations for magazines, textbooks, and books.